Five little women

Unless otherwise indicated, all scripture quotations are taken from the King James Version of the Bible by Thomas Nelson used by permission.

Table of contents

Dedication

To Every dedicated Father and Husband

Acknowledgment

Special Thanks to my family for their support and encouragements throughout this project. God bless you all.

Chapter One

Gone too soon

The best piece of him laid buried in the sands. He and his five daughters paid their last respect to the woman who brought smiles on their faces. It was a quiet funeral. No service of songs, or preacher at the graveside. It was a time of sober reflection, silent sobs and traumatic tears. The sting of death was harsh and the pains that it leaves dampens the soul. Death is a messenger that is deaf to the cry of the innocent and blind to the pleas of loved ones. The only person who had come to mourn with them was Mr. Robin and his sales boy, Bernie. Mr. Robin consoled his friend on the loss of his wife. After much weeping, he led the family to his truck and drove them home. The drive back home was quiet, no one spoke a word. Only the sound of the old truck racketing down the road until it stopped in front of the Smiths' home. It was a little cottage, plastered with cement and furnished with wooden windows and doors.Mr. Smith thanked his friend and went straight to the barn behind the cottage for he wanted to be alone. The girls went inside to mourn for their mother. She was their bedrock and anchor. The poor woman had labored for them all her life and it was quite a tragedy that she had to die in penury. Diane was only seventeen, she was the eldest. Shy and tender like the Lilly plant with lovely dove eyes. She sat on the chair where her mother used to sew clothes thinking about those good times. Julian was fifteen, brave and strongly opinionated. She was fair, beautiful to behold and skillful in all knowledge of science. She sat on a wooden stool and stares at the only picture of their mother on the wall.Betty was only thirteen, she was plump and lovely, very industrious and independent. She stood facing the window, starring at nothing in particular, absent in thought. How she missed her mother! Mariah had just clocked eleven. She was tall and skinny with lovely brown eyes that were strongly captivating. She was a care-free person and always ready to explore new things. She sat on a stool reminiscing those moments she had shared with her beloved mother. Ashley was seven, she was as lovely as the roses of Sharon yet plagued by a mysterious illness from birth. She sat on the floor sobbing until she had no more strength in her. Right there on the floor, she slept off. Diane carried her to the bed and kept her warm. Mr. Smith remained in the barn all day. Mourning and grieving with no one to comfort him.

Chapter Two

Diane elopes

Six months later.

There was a gentle knock at the door.

“who is it? “Diane asked

“It's Bernie.” The voice replied

Diane's heart skipped. He had come to pick up the deliveries. The Smiths had two large diary cows, it was their major source of income. They also had a little poultry and a pig farm.

Diane opened the door, she carried the crate of milk she had kept for sale and passed the crate to Bernie. He paid her and turned around. He made as though he was going to leave but he turned back and asked

“Have you thought about it Diane?” He asked

Diane shook her head. she gave him a negative response.

“Oh Diane, come with me, let's run away and we could be together forever.” he persuaded

“Well, Bernie...I don't...”

“Don’t say that my love. I promise you a life of riches and all the beautiful things you ever wanted.” He whispered to her.

“but ...”

“No buts my love.Our love has no rules. A beautiful damsel as you do not need to milk cows and clean up pens. I promise you a better life.” He persisted

“Okay Bernie.” She said with a wry smile on her face

"Tomorrow, by 8:00 pm, at the motor park. I'll be waiting for you. Love you Diane."

"Love you Bernie." Diane replied and shut the door. She was alone that morning. The other girls had gone to the poultry just behind their house. Diane kept this to herself and secretly began to pack her stuff.

By the eve of the next day, Diane quietly sneaked out of the cottage with few of her belongings. She left a note for her father. She got to the park and found Bernie waiting for her. He had carried some of his luggages too. He hugged her so tight.

"Oh Diane." He whispered and finally let her go "Are you ready?" He asked

"Sure."

He took her to a waiting car and off they went to a new city to start a new life.

Mr. Smith was devastated when he read her note. He had gone to the store to look for Bernie or anyone who knew his whereabouts. Her note left no information about where they had gone to. No postal address and no telephone numbers. The only thing she said was that she was getting married to Bernie and they were moving to a new city.

"Bernie resigned yesterday." Mr. Robin, his boss told him

"Bernie eloped with my daughter." He told Mr. Robin

Mr. Robin looked surprised

"She's only seventeen, she is still a child. How could he run away with my baby girl? Mr. Smith wept.

"Should we notify the local authorities? Mr. Robin said.

" I don't know what to do Robin, I honestly don't know. My heart is broken within me because of Diane, I am like a drunken man and like a man whom wine has overcome." He said

Mr. Smith was just too overwhelmed. He was still grieving the loss of his wife and Diane decided to treat him this way. Mr. Smith thanked Mr. Robin and he went straight to a beer parlor.

He would rather drink away his sorrow than begin a police case.

Chapter Three

Our dreams

"I'm just tired of this life of want and lack." Julian uttered her disgust. "How I wish for a life of ease and plenty. To wear new clothes and adorn my hair beautifully. She made gestures as each sentence fell from her lips. To eat royal dainties, fresh fruits, apples,watermelons,peaches and wine instead of sour milk and frozen fish!. I wish I could be at school hear the bells jingle at break time and at closing time. To be presented love letters and beautiful roses by a charming boy with rounded nose." The girls giggled. I don't know what's it's like to ride home from school or join the school bus and take a stroll with girls down the road. My life is boring, each day, I wake up, work and work. Chatting with pigs and hens and back to more work.Arrgh!" she sighed.

'You know what I want?" Betty asked her sisters but didn't wait for their reply. I want to be a wealthy business woman just like the Dakolo family, Betty said. She's just a successful entrepreneur, a woman of class and style. She exudes radiance each time I see her. I love her life, I wish it was mine." Betty said.

"Then you have to go to Business school but alas! we can't go to school we will never see the four walls of a school." Julian reminded.

"I just want to fulfil my bucket list, travel round the world and write about the beautiful people and their culture that I see." Mariah said. Her sisters chuckled. "Is that all?" Julian asked in disbelief.

"Yes! have breakfast in Paris, lunch in Ethiopia and dinner in Moldova. Isn't that so wonderful?" she asked her sisters. The girls bursted into laughter. "What's so funny?" Mariah asked.

"Your dreams sounds like a day dream, is that all you want from life?" Betty asked.

"Is there more? Mariah asked. I don't want to be strapped with a man who can't take care of his family." she said.

There was silence. Their father came to mind.

"Ashley dear, Julian said what about you? what's your wish?" she asked breaking the silence that lingered.

"I just want to be healthy and happy said the seven years old."

Ashley had been battling a strange illness since birth.

"Aww! my little angel." Betty said.

“She wants all that we have. “Julian remarked. I've been so selfish. She said. we have all been so selfish with our lust and desires. Ashley wants those things money cannot buy.” She patted her little sister on her head. “All will be well.” she said.

“And Diane? what do you think she wanted.” Mariah asked

“She wanted love and to be free and I think she's got it.” Julian said.

“Well, I can't sit here and wish all day. Julian stood up and grabbed her books. I'm going to save more money and sit for the exams and proceed to Nursing school.” She carried her books and stormed out of the house to a quiet place in the barn.

“ I can't be an entrepreneur sitting all day doing nothing.” Betty got up and went to the farm.

“Who’s going to stay with me and teach me now that mother and Diane are gone?” Ashley asked.

“I will dear. come on let's study mathematics together. “Mariah said.

With Diane gone, Betty took over the farming activities. she was a workaholic with great skills. But Julian wanted more out of life. She had dreams of becoming a Nurse at the largest hospital in the town. She worked hard on the farm together with Betty and gathered enough money to go to the city. she knew no one but she was certain when she gets there, fate would make a way for her.

That night, they all say by the lamp. They had only corn for dinner. She told her sisters she was going to the city a couple of weeks from now. The date of the exams into the school of nursing was just a few weeks from now. She was going to stay back in the city until she got admitted into school.

“Diane’s is gone and you too?” Ashley sobbed. Ashley had just recovered once again. Their mother used to treat her with herbs and it only brought temporal relief to her. They were all familiar with the herb their mother boiled and gave Ashley to drink. Once she began to sweat, they knew she was going to be alright.

“But we can't remain like this Ashley. there's nothing graceful about poverty.” Julian said

“But I'm going to miss you.” The little girl said.

“I'm going to visit once in a while. I will write you letters and I will send gifts to you, promise.”

Ashley was soon pacified with the promise of a gift.

Mariah remained quiet. She was the introvert amongst them all and the prettiest.

“Are you not going to say anything?” Julian asked Mariah

“No” she simply bent her head.

Mariah was such a one to bottle her emotions and her pains. She never spoke out. She remained to herself and stayed in doors most time. They never had the privilege of going to school but their mother had home schooled them.

"Well, I'm going to miss you." Julian said to her sister. Mariah simply nodded.

"Have you told father yet?" Betty asked

"No, I don't think he would let me go if I did. but I'll drop a letter for him. Please do well to assure him that I'll always come home, okay Betty?"

"Okay." Betty assured.

Chapter Four

City life

life in the city was better lived than imagined. Sights and sounds were better than pictures, seeing was better than believing, holding and touching was better than imagination. She was fascinated by all she saw in the city. The City bus, the fast life, tall and magnificent buildings, electronic billboards filled her entire view. After an hour at the train station, Julian's mind jolted back to reality. She had to look for a place to stay. She heard that in the city, there were many homeless people. Some people slept on bridges, others under the bridge, many more in uncompleted buildings scattered around the neighborhood, some in school classrooms etc. Although she had saved enough but she doubted if anyone would rent a room for her being a minor. She made up her to go the teaching hospital where she dreamed of becoming a Nurse. She would render her services for free and she hoped she would be given a free accommodation until her admission into the school of nursing was possible. However one thing was certain she wasn't going back home the same way she came.

She asked for directions from a young lady whom she judged to be a student. As Providence would have it, the lady was on her way to the teaching hospital, she was also a medical student. Julian followed her, together they got on a bus to ikejaville and that was the beginning of Julian's journey.

Chapter Five

New beginnings

There was going to be a crusade in town. Its been a month since Julian left for the city. She had not gotten in touch with them. Mr. Smith was very worried. The sorrows and burden of his heart multiplied. First it was his wife, then Diane was married and now Julian. He was scared, not knowing what would happen next. In his desperation, Mr. Smith went to a lonely place, the barn behind his little cottage and cried his heart out. He remembered as a little bit growing up, His mother always took him to church. He was part of the children choir, his mother was a lead choir mistress as well. He heard sermons about a loving God who loved and cared for his people. He had loved the Lord while growing up. But all that changed when his father beat his mother to death. His mother had endured domestic violence all through her marriage. She believed the Lord will change the heart of her husband, but that never happened until he killed her and he was sentenced to life imprisonment. He had to live in a foster home where he was maltreated. He eventually ran away. All this happened when he was only twelve years old. Ever since, he had been fending for himself in a large fruit farm, until at eighteen when he met Elizabeth. It was love at first sight. She made him believe again. Her parents didn't consent to their marriage but Elizabeth left all her beautiful life just to be with him.They went to a small piece of land which her father owned in Seme,where they now lived. Through hard work, they built a little cottage and a barn and farming. He tried to give her a better life but to no avail, until she passed away. He was back in a state of despondency. This time he wanted to Know indeed if God was out there. anywhere.

"Dear God! dear God!! I don't know if you are still out there, if you still do miracles and heal the broken heart. I'm a broken man. I don't know what to do. Twice death has taken the best jewels in my life and now I'm in ruins. help me if you are out there. help me God."

Mr. Smith returned home, looking sad as ever. Betty, Mariah and Ashley were reading one of the books their mother had bought for them. It was five in the evening. There was nothing to eat except a loaf of bread. Mr. Smith, Went into his room and laid on the bed. Just then, there was a knock on the door. Betty opened the door. It was an elderly man flanked by two young men.

"Hello, the elderly man said, his voice hoarse and pleasant.

"Good evening sir." Betty responded

Mr. Smith had come to the front door, Mariah and Ashley soon followed.

"Good day sir." the elderly man greeted Mr. Smith

"Good evening." Mr. Smith replied

"We are from Baptist mission, I'm Evangelist James and these are my pastors Frank and Steve."

Mr. Smith nodded.

"We are having a crusade in this town and we just wanted to invite you and your family. It's starting tonight at the secondary School field. We'll be glad to have you join us." The Evangelist said.

Mr. Smith paused for a while. "Well I will think about it."

"No sir, don't think about it. Jesus is passing by and he says come. So please come." The Evangelist was persuasive

Mr. Smith looked from one preacher to the other, still very uncertain. It's been over twenty five years since he went to church.

"Jesus says come." the Evangelist repeated.

"I will come." Mr. Smith finally said.

"Great, looking forward to seeing you."

They waved goodbye and went their way.

"Dad?" Betty asked

"Yes Betty."

"Are we really going for the crusade?" she asked.

"yes we are."

Chapter Six

Rebirth

Many people had come out for the crusade. The field was packed. On their way, The rumor mill had began to spill again but now it was good news. Stories of the Evangelist has filtered across the little town. They told how he healed the sick and raised the dead and having won millions of souls to the kingdom. They even spoke of how he casted out demons and evil spirits. He was an Evangelist of great repute.

The crusade began with choruses, then with solemn worship. Mr. Smith was familiar with some of those hymns. He remembered singing them while growing up with his mother. Then they sat for a while and listened to wonderful testimonies. The choir came up and gave their anthem before the Evangelist came up the podium.

"The Lord is going to heal broken lives and mend wounded heart. He is going to replace all that has been lost and all that has been stolen. Not only that, He is going to remove sorrows and burden and give fresh beginning. This is what the Lord told he is going to do here tonight and I want you to be prepared because burdens are lifted at Calvary."

Mr. Smith's heart was fixed on the Evangelist. It was as if he heard him in the barn when he prayed. The Evangelist spoke with great power and authority for an hour after which he gave the altar call. Mr. Smith came out, he was overwhelmed with tears and he cried like a baby, He was at the front, on his knees. He and others were led into the sinners prayer and there he gave his life to Christ. He was now born again.

Mr. Smith's heart was filled with joy. He couldn't explain the joy that welled up within him. He returned to his seat and for the first he hugged his daughters. They didn't understand what had happened to their father but they saw a changed man and his face looked radiant.

The following night was even more glorious. The Evangelist was on the move, binding and casting out evil spirits. He moved in the midst, laying hands on the people. Some staggered and others fell. Mr. Smith found himself on the floor after the Evangelist laid his hands on him. When he woke up after the crusade, almost every one had gone home.

"Father, are you alright?" Mariah asked

"Oh yes! I'm fine. He stood up and removed the dust from his clothes. what happened?" He asked

"You fell under the power of God I suppose." Betty offered a suggestion.

"Oh did I? He teased

"Dad!" the girls chuckled

"Come on let's go home." He said

Mr. Smith became a different man.He hugged his girls every morning and told them he loved them. From that day on, he woke up each morning with this same chorus

"This joy that I have, the world didn't give it to me

this joy that I have, the world didn't give it to me

this joy that I have, the world didn't give it to me,

the world didn't give it, the world can't take it away."

The girls joined him in the chorus and it was such a happy time in the family again. He helped the girls in the farm and things were looking good again. Sales increased and they were able to take care of their needs. Mr. Smith wished the crusade would never end. Tonight was the seventh day, the last day and the Evangelist had said he was going to speak on the Holy Spirit.

As ever before, the field was packed and the atmosphere was beautiful. More testimonies, healing and deliverance. The Evangelist gave his sermon on the Holy spirit and asked those who wanted to be filled to come forward. Mr. Smith came forward and after prayers and laying on of hands, he spoke with a new tongue. But something even more spectacular happened. Betty was also baptized in the Holy spirit and spoke with new tongues.

Chapter Seven

The call

Something changed. That was all they knew!

Their father woke them up each morning and they prayed as a family and worked together as a family. Mr. Smith went to his old box and there he found his Bible. it was old and dusty, he had not touched it in years. They began to read the Bible together and they prayed together even in the holy ghost. The sales in their business tripled and they could afford a better life style. New clothing and shoes and they expanded their business.

At midnight, Mr. Smith would wake up to pray for his daughters Diane and Julian. That the Lord will keep them. He wanted to see his daughters again specially Diane. he prayed earnestly for them, he did so day and night. But Mr. Smith had been having strange dreams lately. He always saw himself catching fish. Could it be he should go into fishing business? He wasn't so sure. After weeks of having the same dream, he decided to write a letter to the Evangelist about it. After several weeks of waiting, A young man came knocking at their door one afternoon. He had a letter in his hand. He was from the Evangelist. Mr. Smith was very glad to receive the reply. He thanked the bearer and went to his room to read the letter

Beloved,

Blessed be the name of God forever. For wisdom and might are his. Your dreams are one. God has shown you great favor and mercy and had called you into the ministry. To be a Fisher of men, to do the work of an Evangelist. This is what the dreams means. I encourage you to fast and pray so as to get instructions from the Holy spirit that you may begin your ministry speedily.

May the grace of our Lord Jesus Christ remain with you. Amen

Yours in Christ

James.

How could he leave all and become a Fisher of men? an Evangelist? Mr. Smith was really confused. A fortnight later, the Evangelist Pastor James came himself. Without much talk, he anointed Mr. Smith and did some impartation upon him. Mr. Smith was on the floor again. He invited Mr. Smith to follow him as a start. He being fully persuaded bided his daughters farewell. He would go on crusades and come back to his family. That was the plan. The Evangelist prayed with his daughters and encouraged them to remain fervent and steadfast in His grace. So Mr. Smith began to follow Evangelist James in his ministry, moving from town to town and cities to cities preaching the gospel of Jesus.

Chapter Eight

Christmas with a difference

It was Christmas season. Julian got out of the cab and stood in front of the little cottage.

She couldn't believe her eyes. this was not the same house she had left over a year ago. She almost thought she was lost but the barn behind the cottage was the only clue left. she was certain this was home. The cottage had been repainted with wine color. A Christmas tree had been mounted outside the house and Christmas light around the tree and at the entrance of the house. It was a breathtaking view. Just then the door flung open. Mariah stood at the door.

"Julian! she screamed excitedly. Betty and Ashley ran to the door. Julian was still standing at the gate. The girls ran to her and hugged her tightly one after the other.

"look at you! Betty exclaimed you look like a city girl." she remarked. Julian wore a pink fitted gown with high heels and her hair were neatly braided.

"How are you all doing? you all look well Julian said How's father?" she asked

Just then Mr. Smith stood at the front door.

"Father! Julian said and ran into her fathers embrace.

"Oh Julian! Julian!" he said a tear streaming down his cheek.

"Father! she said you look great what happened. everything looks wonderful."

"Yes! yes! there's been a great change Julian, come inside and let's talk about it."

Julian re capped all that had happened to her at the city, how she met Crystal, a medical student at the train station. It was Crystal that took her in and cared for her after she narrated her story to her and told her she had no place to go. Crystal was a Christian and she took pity on her. She also helped her to prepare for the forth coming exams which she passed with flying colors. The school gave the best student a partial scholarship to the school of nursing. They all listened with rapt attention and were filled with excitement.

Her father broke the news that he was now an Evangelist. He told her how God changed his life and gave him a ministry and saved him from depression and drunkenness. He could Meet his needs and provide for the family. They were all very happy once again.

"This is the best Christmas in a long time." Mr. Smith said. God has answered my prayer request. He has seen my tears and heard my supplications. This is one of the best Christmas gift and I know that he will grant all my heart desires."

Julian asked if they had heard from Diane. There had been no word from her neither does anyone know her whereabouts. But Mr. Smith committed everything into God's hands.

It was five days to Christmas and Mr. Smith gave the girls money for shopping. They had never shopped for Christmas clothes, shoes and food like this for many years. They were so excited it was indeed like a dream when the Lord turned around their captivity. They now had a plasmaTV, a sound system new upholstery, beautiful paper walls in the living room and in the bedroom. They had brought Christmas carols and Christmas movies. Christmas day was even more glorious. They attended church service and the neighbors were very warm and kind to them. They exchange gifts and food and took pictures together. In the evening, fireworks were on display and everything looked beautiful. They had watched the nativity of Jesus at church, the drama group had staged a play on the birth of Jesus. While the girls enjoyed themselves, Mr. Smith prayed earnestly for Diane to return home. soon, it was new year and the new year was greeted with fireworks and celebration but for Mr. Smith and his family, they prayed into the new year, committing the year into God's hands and their own lives.By the second week of the new year, Julian returned back to school. Mr. Smith was also going for several new year crusades which the Evangelist had invited him for. He was going to be away from his daughters for two weeks. He was happy to serve the Lord but sad he had to be away from them for such a long time but he committed all things to the hands of God by prayer.

Chapter Nine

Diane's troubles

It was a different life. It was a hard life and Diane was a stranger to it. Early morning sickness, days without a decent meal, no one to chat with, no radio, no television and no visits. She sat in a corner and wept sore. How she wished she could see her sisters again and her father. At least in her father's house, she could boast of a meal every day. She could be in a lively company, stroll around the compound and fall asleep on a couch or on her bed. But life with Bernie wasn't any bed of roses as he made her to believe. She was faced with reality, startled by facts. Life is not for the wishy washy, the faint hearted, not even for the shy ones. The Swift ones could overcome, the strong could overcome but only the violent ones, taketh it by force and Diane was not of such breed. She was such a gentle and shy girl, an alien to city life especially this life of couple living. Bernie got a job in a beverage factory company. He worked from 8am Until 6pm and his salary could only feed one mouth. Transportation and electricity bill took half of his wages. He could barely cope with the pressure of family, this was not what he had planned. Bernie had a friend in the factory called Scott. Scott introduced him into Sports betting where he could make extra earnings. Bernie was skeptical at first but after a win in his first attempt, Bernie got hooked on betting. Sometimes he won and other times he lost. His betting habit took away his salary each month. Soon he started borrowing money from his colleagues until he ran into debts. This made Bernie to stay away from his home because his creditors came with police officers to arrest him. Diane was able to start home lessons in order to take care of herself but each time she saved up money, the creditors came and she gave it to them. Diane hated her life, she hated herself for leaving all behind and venturing into a life of misery and uncertainty with Bernie.

In moments like this, she wished her mother was alive. Now her mind raced in different directions. To kill herself? or go back home? to remain quiet and suffer? She didn't have the slightest clue of what to do? Is this what married life was all about? She had seen her parents in the home. Though they had no money, they were very happy together but her story with Bernie was not the same. The young man who wrote her love letters and promised her a life of bliss and roses had suddenly become her worst nightmare. Sometimes she wished he never came home, if he did, he was going to treat her badly or take all her money. Things had really gone so bad. Now she realized that love doesn't put food on the table or pay the bills. Love gave no guarantee to a happy marriage if the couples didn't work together as a team. She realized that love without communication or trust was worthless. Wished she had known these things before she eloped with Bernie. She would never had made this decision. She felt trapped, unloved and unhappy. Bernie had become like a deaf cobra that stops it's ear, which will not heed the voice of charmers, charming ever so skillfully. He wouldn't listen to his friend Scott who advised him to take things easy.Bernie was now hooked on drugs and women. He had forgotten the promises he made to Diane his first love and had gone after other women. He left his tender vine and went after wild grapes and they turned his heart completely away from Diane for she meant nothing to him anymore.

Chapter Ten

Family first

Mariah had gone to the liquor store and bought some vodka. She had invited two other girls whom she met at the last Christmas for a sleepover party while her father had gone for a crusade. Betty scolded her for such an act but Mariah cared less. At 6pm, her new friends Sonia and Alice arrived. They had also brought porn movies with them and some pop corn too. But Betty would have none of it. The fracas continued until there was a gentle knock at the door. Betty opened the door, to their greatest surprise, it was their father.

"Father!" Mariah said with utmost surprise in her voice. Her friends stood up and quickly rushed out of the door. A gentleman had followed their father, he carried his luggages.

"What is going on here?" he asked

"Nothing father." Mariah lied

"Father, Betty began, Mariah brought in strangers here and she also has some booze with her." His eyes widened. He stared at Mariah. Mariah didn't utter a word, she only bent her head low.

" Is that so Mariah?" her father asked

"Fatherl Ashley came out of the room and hugged her father.

"How are you doing pumpkin?" He carried her in his arms. She was in her nighties and already feeling sleepy.

"Great!" she said. He put her down and thanked the young man who had helped him. "Clear this spare room Betty please and young lady, he said pointing at Mariah follow me to my room. This is Pastor Timothy. He will be joining me in my crusades and revival meetings." Mr. Smith said

"Pastor Tim, these are my daughters, Betty, Mariah and Ashley. Julian is in nursing school,you will meet her pretty soon." He said

The girls welcomed him and led him to the small store which Dad had converted to his study room. There was a small bed there for him and there he made himself comfortable.

Evangelist sat on his bed, Mariah was standing at the entrance of the door. She was too scared to come closer, she didn't know what her father would do to her.

Mr. Smith had a change of heart and came home earlier than the schedule time. Evangelist James had warned him of the danger of leaving his family behind in ministry. Evangelist James told him his family was his first ministry and if he failed in training his children in the way they ought to go, it didn't matter the miracles, signs and wonders he did out there, he was still a failure.

Those words stucked on him. He had failed his daughters once but God in his mercies gave him a second chance and he wasn't about to screw up. He cancelled his next meeting and came home just to find Mariah on the verge of making a big mistake.

" Sit." he said, patting the bed beside him.

Slowly, Mariah sat beside him.

"Mariah dear, there's a way that seems right to teenagers but the end is destruction. Darling, I want you to understand that the devil is after your soul and the soul of Everyman just to destroy them and do you know how he does that? "he asked

"No father, how?"

"By enticing them to sin, By deception, by encouraging them to obey their lust and when sin takes hold, it becomes an addiction and you can't break free. It makes you a slave just like it did to me.But remember that song

Jesus sets me free, why should I be bound

Jesus sets me free, why should I e bound

Jesus sets me free, why should I be bound

why should I be bound.

"Jesus has made you free and you are free indeed. Mariah, don't obey your lust and your flesh, flee from sin and resist it's temptations okay?

"Okay father." She managed a smile.

"Let's pray together. He said and so Mr. Smith prayed with his daughter and she went to bed. He had a light dinner of spaghetti, grilled fish and tomato sauce with orange juice with Timothy. After dinner, he retired to his room. He knew exactly what to do hence forth. Mr. Smith had called Mr. Robin. He was going to rent his home and his little farm while he travelled with his daughters for his ministrations. He believed the Lord will take care of their tomorrow for the Lord was their tomorrow. When the deal was completed, he travelled with his daughters. They had packed all their stuff to a corner in the barn, rented out the farm and his cottage. Hence forth he travelled with his daughters. They will stay briefly at the mission house and move on until the Lord granted them rest. Right now, his next stop was Yorkville

Chapter Eleven

Another fight

Mr. Smith had been invited to a crusade at Yorkville. The crusade had been widely publicized and the whole town was looking forward to it. It was a six weeks long crusade. The people brought the blind, the lame, the paralyzed and all that were sick and afflicted with diseased and all they were demonized. Smith came with his son in the ministry, Timothy who waited on him. He met Timothy at his last crusade. Timothy was a nephew to Evangelist James. He was only Twenty one. He had been following the Evangelist since he was sixteen. His mother Lois and grandmother Georgia were devout Christians. Timothy had been born after twelve years of barreness,hence his mother Lois made a vow to return him back to the Lord. Evangelist James was old and retiring from the Ministry, so he handed Timothy to Mr. Smith. Mr. Smith quickly adopted him as a son in the ministry and together, they began their Evangelist ministry after walking with Evangelist James for a year. Together, they prepared for a six weeks revival meeting here in Yorkville as directed by the Holy Spirit.

It was 11pm, there was knock on the door.

"Diane,Diane,open the door." Bernie's voice jolted Diane out of her sleep.

"Bernie? is it you?" she asked

"Yes, open the door."

Diane stood up from the old tattered mattress, lighted a candle and opened the door. Bernie rushed in and locked the door. He was smelling of booze and cigarettes.

"Bernie? have you been drinking again? Diane asked in a quiet voice. Bernie took off his booths and socks. He sat on the Sofa. The sofa had no cloth, only tattered foams on the wooden structure.

"Why are you monitoring me woman?" He snorted back

There was a brief silence.

"The creditors came again." She began but Bernie cut her off

Did you give them some money?"

"Yes I did..but"

"That's fine." He said

“But Bernie we can't continue like this! I'm tired of this kind of life. This is not what you promised me.”

Bernie got up, breathing hard, he walked up to her, his eyes as red as crimson.

“Are you calling me a liar? or a failure? you good for nothing bitch!" Bernie hit her hard and she fell to the ground. He kicked her stomach as hard as he could. Diane let out a cry of pain. Bernie put on his booths, opened the door and stormed out of the house again as it was his usual habit. Diane winced in pain all through the night.

Chapter Twelve

Mrs. Potter

It was the second week of the crusade and God had crowned each meeting with miracles, signs and wonders. After the meeting. The pastorate gathered around Mr. Smith they had a brown envelope in their hands. The senior pastor of Great revival ministry thanked him once again.

"That was a wonderful ministration sir. more grace and anointing." He said presenting the envelope to him.

"Thank you, you are most kind." He said accepting the envelope from him.

"Sir, there's a sister who is very ill. She is such a wonderful philanthropist in this town. She helps the widow, the orphans and supports the ministry. She's a widow and a devoted Christian, she would have been here for the crusade. Please can you come over and pray with her."

"Off course, where does she lives?" He asked

"Not too far away, we can drive there in my car." he replied.

"Okay then he said, handing over the envelope to Timothy." Timothy collected it, picked his Bible and his coat and followed Mr. Smith behind.

They drove to the sister's house. She lived in a Porsche area in the neighborhood. She was very wealthy and influential. Her house sat on a Five acre piece of land with lush green grasses, a mansion with a garage full of cars. She also has a guest house where she lodged in visitors. The entire view was breath-taking. The elder parked in front of the house. A maid stepped out to receive them.

"She's waiting upstairs." she announced to them.

The senior pastor, Mr. Smith and Timothy went up to her room. She laid on the bed, unable to speak or to stand up. Mr. Smith prayed for her, laid his hands on her and walked away. The maid thanked them and returned. The trio went back into the car, they have barely driven out of the garage when the maid ran out of the house and began to chase the car.

"Stop! He said to the senior pastor look, the maid is running after us."Mr. Smith said

The senior pastor stopped and the maid came closer.

"Mrs. Potter, she's talking, she wants you back. please come back." the maid said panting after each sentence.

"Well! praise the Lord? what a speedy miracle." said the senior pastor. Shall we go back? he asked Mr. Smith

"Sure we can." he said and they drove back to the house.

She was in the living room when they returned. The senior pastor was shocked to see her alive and full of strength.

she rose to greet the group and offered them a seat.

"Thank you Pastor and thank you Evangelist for coming." Said Mrs. Potter

"Thank God for his mercies." Mr. Smith said.

"I wanted to host you and to thank you Evangelist she began. Thank you man of God."

"The glory belongs to God." Mr. Smith remarked.

"I hear that you are currently in the mission house with your family sir. If you would honour me sir, I will be glad if you come stay in the guest house with your family for the next couple of weeks of your crusade." She pleaded.

"That's most kind of you." Mr. Smith said but I'm fine and...

"Please sir, if you judge me a faithful servant please come over, it's very comfortable for you sir."

Mr. Smith looked at the senior pastor he was only beaming with smiles.

"Well, I will talk to the committee about it and let you know." Mr. Smith said.

She offered them lunch but Mr. Smith insisted of taking water only. They thanked her and went on their way.

Chapter Thirteen

Turnaround

Diane suffered a third miscarriage and Bernie didn't return home that night either. By morning, Diane was weak. She managed to get up and clean herself and the floor. Tired and exhausted with nothing to eat, she decided to end it all. At twelve noon, Bernie came home with a prostitute and took her into their matrimonial room. When she tried to object, Bernie gave her another beating. She laid on the bare floor, bleeding through her nose. They went inside and made love to each other. The cries and pleasure of the prostitute ringing and reverberating across the room tore Diane heart out. This was torture, this was enough, she was going to kill herself, she was going to end it once and for all. She got out of the house and ran to train station. It was not busy as usual. She sat on a wooden bench waiting for a train to come and she would jump in and end it all. An elderly lady came by and sat beside Diane. Diane had not taken notice of the woman. She was lost in her thoughts, weeping only waiting for the train to come.

"You know, I am going to see my son." the old lady began

"It's been sixteen years since I last saw him. I went into prostitution and abandoned him when he was ten. He needed me but I was too selfish because I wanted to enjoy my life."

Diane looked at the elderly woman, uninterested in her story but she kept quiet.

"But life treated me unfairly and now I'm suffering from a terminal disease. I don't have much time to live but I realize that the only thing I want right now is to reconcile with my son." She said.

"I couldn't forgive myself for what I did to him but instead he forgave me and told me he wants to see me. He wants me to spend the few time I have left with him." Tears began to flow from her eyes.

"I thank God for this second chance because he is a God of second chance. I thank God I didn't take my life when things were so bad." She looked into Diane's eyes.

"No matter how bad it has been, God gives us a second chance." The old lady said. Just then the train arrived. The old lady got in and waved to Diane. Diane didn't wave back. Her words filtered into her mind. She didn't notice when the train arrived. She had completely forgotten what she came here for.

Second chance, second chance. She could ask God to give her a second chance and maybe her father too would give her a second chance. She stood up and decided to go for the crusade in town.Diane arrived at the venue by 8pm.The choir just began and after their ministration, the Evangelist came on. It was her father. Right there at the altar, she could see Betty, Mariah and Ashley but there was no sight of Julian. She wept realizing how much she missed them and how wrong she was to have left without saying goodbye. The message began, again it was titled the prodigal son. Diane couldn't hold back her tears, throughout the sermon she was weeping. Then Mr. Smith gave the altar call and many people came out and gave their heart to Christ. He prayed for them all. He prayed for the sick and healed them all, he also prayed for the oppressed and the Lord delivered them all. After all was said and done, he brought the service to a close, it was already 10p.m. Every one was making their way out of the church but Diane went to the altar, knelt down, covered her face and wept. She remained there for thirty minutes. Everyone had left except the Senior pastor, Timothy and the Evangelist. The girls left with Mrs. Potter also. They all wondered what was wrong with the lady. Finally Timothy was asked to Minister to her.

"Hello sister, please rise." he said

Diane raised her head, tried to clean her bruised face.

"It's okay, it's okay. He said. Our pastors wants to pray with you." He said motioning her to where they stood. At that moment, their eyes met and she froze. She missed a heart beat, her stomach tightened, her hands shaking. Here she was, face to face with her father, uncertain of his reaction.

"Diane!" The words fell out of Mr. Smith's lips. He was trembling and sweating. He began to weep. Now he could see her bruised face and how malnourished and unkempt she was.

"Diane!" He repeated. This time, walking towards her. Diane covered her face with her palm and wept even more. This time, he was standing right in front of her, his hands opened and he called out the third time with a loud voice weeping "Diane my child." This time, she ran into his embrace and they both wept sore. The pastorate watched, amazed at what they saw.

Chapter Fourteen

The reunion

The drive home was very quite. Diane was surprised when they got to the guest house. She had never seen such an exquisite apartment. Out came Mrs. Potter to receive him. The Evangelist introduce Diane to Her as his daughter and she was elated. Thanking and praising God. They went inside the house. As Diane stepped in, her sisters stopped dead. Not believing their eyes but their father said to them.

"It's Diane!"

The girls rushed to their elder sister and hugged her tightly. No one saying a word, only soft sobs and cries filled the entire space. After a long while,Mrs. Potter took Diane to the main house to care for her and nurse her bruises. Mr. Smith sat outside the guest house weeping and thanking God while he shared his testimony with Senior Pastor and Timothy. It was past 10:00pm but no one felt sleepy or tired. The mood was that of joy, tears of joy.Mrs Potter invited everyone to the main house for dinner for they had neither ate nor drank since they returned from the Meeting. Diane had changed into a plain silver dinner gown, her hair neatly packed and her bruises cared for. She looked elegant, not as the broken girl who wept at the altar few hours ago. Mrs. Potter had prepared chicken broth for the first course meal. For the main course they ate risotto and duck meat and for dessert, they had vanilla cakes and ice cream. It was a warm and happy reunion. No one went back to the past, they were filled with praises to God. After desert, They bade Mrs. Potter goodnight and returned to the guest house. Timothy and the Senior Pastor returned to the mission house. One after the other, the girls went to bed but Diane remained in the living room with her father. He could see she was tired and exhausted. Diane was still feeling uneasy, she was yet to free herself but her father led her to one of the furnished rooms.

"This is your bedroom my dear." he said

"All for me? she said looking at the stylish room with beautiful wall papers, lampstands and curtains."

"Yes my dear, feel free and enjoy yourself." he said

da..dad! she said

"Yes?"

"Where's Julian?" She asked

"Julian is in nursing school at Ikejaville."

“Oh! that's lovely.” Diane remarked

“Now go to bed, it's been a long day.” He sat beside her on the bed, held her hands and prayed with her.

“Goodnight he said and planted a kiss on her forehead.”

“Goodnight Dad.” Diane replied.

He walked out of the room, shut the door behind him and tears streamed down his face. His heart was full of gratitude. God has answered his prayers yet again.

Chapter Fifteen

The dream

It was the third time Mr. Smith was having this same dream. He called the pastors together for an urgent meeting. They met at the conference room in the church. the meeting had been scheduled for 2pm. The elders, the Senior Pastor, Timothy and the Evangelist were present. It was a sunny afternoon. Each man with his handkerchief, cleaning his sweat. They began the meeting with prayers. one of the elders prayed.

Heavenly father we thank you for gathering us together in unity. So we commit our meeting into your hands, let it be fruitful and we will give you all the glory. Amen

"Amen." They all said

"Well, thank you for coming. I called this meeting because of something that burdens my heart. He looked at each elder, cleared his throat and continued. I've been here for four weeks and you have hosted me and my family and I must say thank you. And my gratitude also to Mrs. Potter. But lately I've had this dream three times. I was driving a car, going about my evangelism with my daughters in the car and I met this woman standing by the road. She was the only passenger there. I picked her up and we went together. The second dream, I refused to pick her up and got a punctured tyre. I couldn't go anywhere. He stopped looked again at the faces of the elders. This woman is Mrs. Potter." he finished.

The senior pastor cleared his throat, he smiled and asked the Evangelist. "Do you understand the interpretation of the dream?"

He paused. "Yes I do." he said finally.

"Then it's clear enough what the will of God is Evangelist." said the pastor.

"How do I tell this woman? How will God join me with a woman I'm not even in love with?" he asked

"Are you questioning God?" they asked

"No but..."

"No buts Mr. Smith. Pray about it and talk to this woman. You have our support." They said.

"But I'm set to leave in two weeks time." he said.

"Then postpone your meeting and settle this matter. Take as long as you want. Then you can be sure to proceed with or without her in your evangelism." They said.

"Fair enough." Mr. Smith said and thanked them.

Three days after, Mr. Smith invited Mrs. Potter to the office.Mr. Smith thanked her for coming on quite a short notice. The Pastorate had persuaded him to speak to her as soon as possible and not to delay.

Mr. Smith narrated his dream to her and asked what she thought. She told him she would pray about it. They decided to give themselves to prayer and more prayers and converge after two weeks.

Two weeks seemed like two years before the Evangelist. The days dragged and the night lingered so long. He didn't understand why he had become so anxious like a young boy waiting to get a yes. He had also changed his looks these days. He became more conscious of his looks and appearance. He had told his daughters about his dream and all. They were praying he would get a yes. Over the past weeks, they have grown fond of Mrs. Potter and couldn't imagine saying goodbye to her. How lovely it will be to have her as a step mother. She had guided Diane through those difficult moments and Diane was back to her lovely self though still shy but she was free with everyone and herself. After two weeks, they had arranged to meet by 6pm again in the pastor's office. If she gave him a no, he had made up his mind to leave with his daughters first thing tomorrow but for now, he must wait to get a yes. They sat opposite each other, after Mr. Smith had said a short prayer, he paused and cleared his throat.

'What do you say to my proposal Mrs. Potter. Mr. Smith said, in a cool calm tone which he had rehearsed over and over so as not to let his anxiety show.

She looked up and gave a smile. "It's a yes." she said.

Chapter Sixteen

The union

Julian rushed home as soon as she got the news. Diane was back home and her father was getting married again! This must be crazy! Their lives were about to change three hundred and sixty degrees forever! The girls learned that Mrs. Potter was married to a wealthy real estate mogul. They had no child together until he passed away after a brief illness, five years after their marriage. Mrs. Potter had promised never to marry again, only to serve the Lord and use her wealth to promote good. Mrs. Potter was an elderly woman who just clocked fifty. She was seven years younger than Mr. Smith. Julian once again started the chatter. “Wow! My life will become so easy and beautiful she gushed! I don't have to work so hard to pay my tuition, I can now wear beautiful satin and silk clothes, make beautiful hair and maybe get a small car!” she gushed

“You wish! Betty laughed. Now I can go to Business school like the Dakolo's and become a boss lady someday.” Betty said.

“You are not tired of competing with Mrs. Dakolo?” Julian asked

“No way. That woman's life is pretty and easy and until my life is pretty and easy, I won't give up the chase.” Betty said.

“And I will just keep travelling round the world, taking beautiful photographs all over.” Mariah announced.

“They all chuckled. That’s not a big dream!” Julian teased

“But it's what I want.” Mariah defended

“Let her be! Betty said she's on her way to discover another Victoria water fall.” She teased.

“And you bet, I will.” Mariah said

“And you Ashley? Julian asked again

“I want to celebrate my birthday in a big way in good health.” Ashley said

“awwh! Don't worry pumpkin. you will be just fine.” Julian assured.

They looked at Diane who had been quiet but had been giggling along.

"What about you Diane" Julian asked.

She looked at her sisters and said " I just want a second chance to do things right again." she said.

"Stamped! Julian said It shall be as you have spoken."

Six months later, Mr. Smith was married to Mrs. Potter. Timothy was the best man and Diane the maid of honor. And all the girls formed the bridal train. It was a quiet wedding and they were joined by the senior pastor of the church.Mrs Potter insisted they moved into the main house and live like one big happy family.

The new couple travelled to Kenya for their honeymoon. They wanted a safari theme honeymoon and the girls were very happy and grateful to God for everything. The newly Weds spent a month in Kenya. Pastor Timothy and Diane became very close friends. He held Bible study with her and she also became his prayer partner. They were growing into best friends in the church and in the neighborhood. After a month, Mr. and Mrs. Smith Returned home and the girls were elated to see their father and their new mother.

Chapter Seventeen

The talk

One morning, Diane stood, admiring the portrait of her father's wedding photo in the living room. Her father walked in and saw her admiring it. He had never talked to her about her marriage with Bernie.He wanted to give her time to recover and be part of the family again. He cleared his throat, Diane looked back, startled to know that she has not been alone all this while.

"Father, good morning. I thought you were already in the church office." she stammered

"I'm on my way dear." he responded

"Where's mum?" she asked further

"She took Ashley for check up. They have an appointment." he said

"Oh, I see. breakfast?" Diane asked

"No dear, no breakfast for me. Diane, come have a seat." Mr. Smith said pointing to a chair beside him. Diane sat beside her father. He took her right hand in his left hand and spoke softly.

"Tell me dear, what happened when you left with Bernie? Did you get married legally?" Mr. Smith asked

Diane had known fully well that this conversation would come up someday. Now was the perfect time, she had healed up and she was ready to speak.

"Well father, Bernie promised me a better life and made me believe that life was a bed of roses. He told me we could settle in a far away city with no worries, we will be free and happy and I wanted to be happy." she said

her father nodded his head

" We eloped that night to this city Yorkville. We were never married but he introduced me to everyone in the town as his wife and I felt it was okay. He got a miniflat and a decent job but I stayed at home, he didn't want me to work." She paused

"Go on dear." her father said

“We could barely meet our needs. He went into betting, drinking and hard drugs. Soon he ran into debts and hardly came home. I started teaching and saving up money but the creditors took it away. Bernie would beat me and starve me and bring harlots into our home. It was a harrowing experience father. Tears streamed her face. I would be hungry for days, thrice I had miscarriages. So I decided to end my life.”

“What changed your mind?” her father asked

“I met a woman who shared her story with me right there at the train station.” she said. Thank God I listened to her.” She paused and looked at her Dad. “Father, I'm very sorry for letting you down...”

“No Diane, no my dear, I’m the one who let you down. Its my fault that I didn't step up and be a father to my children. I allowed my circumstance to weigh me down and I was losing control of my home and children. But I thank God for a second chance to make everything right again.” He pulled her closer.

“God will give you a second chance and a new beginning my dear. Old things are passed away and behold all things will become new.” Her father assured her.

“Thank you father.”

“So what's your plan? What do you want to do now?” her father asked

“I want to pray about it father.” she said

“Take your time dear. This is your home and I want you around me okay? Her father said

“Okay father.”

“I must be on my way now.”

“Father?”

“Yes”

“Can I walk with you down to church?”

“Yes you may my dear.” I have a prophetic retreat coming up today. Let’s go and plan together. He looked at Diane’s face. They laughed, stood up and walked out of the door together.

Chapter Eighteen

Timothy's thought

The prophetic retreat was powerful. Men of God from across the state converged for the meeting.This was the first time Mr. Smith had given Timothy the opportunity to Minister and he had done excellently well. Timothy had served him faithfully for the past two years and he loved him as a son because he waited on him all day long.One day, the two men had Bible study together and prayed together. Mr. Smith invited him to lunch for they had been fasting since morning. Timothy obliged and they walked home together. They sat at the balcony while Mrs. Smith prepared the meal. The girls had gone to their various schools. They were alone.

"Sir, There's something I would like to tell you." Timothy began.

"Go on Timothy, what is it?"

"Sir, I have been praying concerning my marital life and I'm fully persuaded that your daughter, Diane is God's will for me." He paused, looked at Mr. Smith but his face was blank without any expression.

"I have come to you as a father in the Lord for counseling and advice before I approach her." Timothy said.

It took a while before Mr. Smith responded.

"And what are those things that convinced you." he asked.

"Well sir, actually the first time I saw her, a seven months ago, the holy spirit said to me, that's the lady. But I needed more signs and more convictions." said.

"And did you get them?" Mr. Smith asked

"Yes sir I did. During that prophetic retreat, one of the prophet spoke specific words to me not to judge her but accept her Scarlet and he would make it white as snow. I was discouraged by her past at first but the Lord has helped me and now, I love her." he said.

Mr. Smith remained quiet. "Well, Timothy, when the Lord speaks, we have to obey. If you are fully persuaded, then you should pray to God for the right place and time to speak to her."

"I will do that sir." He said. Timothy looked up and finally he spoke. "And you sir? are you fine with it?"

Mr. Smith laughed. “Let’s do God's will first, okay?”

“Yes sir.”

Just then, Betty, Mariah and Ashley arrived from school. Betty was having an altercation with the driver. Mr. Smith and Timothy were laughing. Mrs. Smith and Diane stepped out into the balcony to announce that lunch was served.

“And what's so funny? Mrs. Smith asked

“Betty got spiritual with the driver.” They said

“He was driving like Jehu, with reckless abandon and I had to go into the spirit to caution him.” Betty said as she came close to them.

They all laughed “She's just too spiritual.” Said Mr. Smith. “Come inside let's all have lunch. Timothy will be joining us.” he said.

Chapter Nineteen

Questions

Diane sat at the last pew. She had been watching her Father who had been counselling and praying for some members that waited after the evening service. Mother and the girls had gone home but there was a burden in Diane's heart she wanted to share.

“Good night Sister Diane.” the last person waved. It was the chief usher, Deacon Sam.

“Good night Deacon.” she responded in her soft voice.

Her father had walked down to where she sat with his big king James giant print Bible in his right hand. He took his seat beside her, closing the distance between them.

“So young lady, he began what's the burden in your heart.” He said not as a father but as a Pastor

Diane chuckled. “Well, I just wanted to know how would a young girl know her soul mate? How would I know he is God's will for me?” She began

Mr. Smith cleared his throat. “Well first of all, God begins to speak to you about little things then about big things. Like the weather, or what's going to happen next, who is coming and what the day will be like. Then he moves to big things like his plans and purpose for you, for his people etc.”

“How and when does God speaks?” Diane asked

“At first, he speaks through his word. Then he speaks through his servants the prophets and then in audible small voice and also through dreams.”

“I've been having a particular dream lately.” she said.

“Tell me about it.”

“I usually see myself wearing a new beautiful shoe and it fits perfectly.” she said

“Shoes in the dream for an unmarried woman signifies marriage. God is telling you he has prepared a wonderful soul mate for you and it's time you consider marriage.” he said

Diane remained silent.

“Has anyone proposed to you yet?” her father asked.

"No, sir. no one yet." She said

"Okay let's pray together." He prayed for her after that, he turned off the lights and locked up the church and they headed home.

"My dear, her father began. I think Timothy is a fine young man, responsible and one with a genuine call of God upon his life." Diane looked startled. So her father had known all along and he remained quiet. "I know he will make you happy and together you can both fulfil God's plan and purpose for your lives. I know he truly loves you and I'm more than willing to accept him as a son in law." he paused and looked straight into her eyes.

"Do you love him too?" he asked

"Yes father but you know I once made a mistake.."

"My dear, with God there are no mistakes but promises fulfilled. He is yes and amen to our desires that are according to his will. Don't let your past block the riches of his grace and mercy. let go and let God. okay?"

"Yes father."

"Speaking of which you need faith like that young lady over there." He pointed at Betty. They both laughed.

"I need a Betty kind of faith."

"Yes we all need a Betty kind of faith.'

Betty met her father and Diane at the door entrance.

"How's it going Betty?" her father asked

"Oh father, every promise in the book is mine. Every line and every verse is mine. My beginning may be small but my latter end will greatly increase." Betty said.

"Preach it!" Her father said

"I will sit with kings and not with mean men for my talents and gifts will furnish a room for me and my head will lack no oil." Betty winced and spoke in unknown tongues

Great! I join my faith with yours." her father said "won't you Diane?"

"Of course, I join my little faith with yours also." Diane said. They all laughed knowing Diane had no faith at all.

Chapter Twenty

The wedding

But Ashley's sickness kept recurring. Mr. Smith didn't understand why people who came to the meetings, old, young, men, women boys and girls were healed but Ashley's case still remained the same. Her parents decided to hold special prayers for her everyday. Seeking God's mercy and favor with fasting and prayers for her. The elders and pastors joined them praying earnestly and without season, continually for her. Ashley recovered soon. There was absolute no medical explanation for her illness. It happened at a specific date in each month and lasted for ten days. That had been the norm since she was born until now.

Timothy after much prayers popped the question to Diane. Diane was elated and gave him a yes. He had bought an emerald heart shaped engagement ring for her and she loved it.

Timothy joined Mr. Smith and his family on Sundays after service for brunch. However, this time, he had a special announcement to make. Mrs. Smith made barbeque and cocktail for every one. It was such a wonderful family time. After much drinking and eating, Timothy cleared his throat and said.

"I've a special announcement to make." He smiled. His left hand holding Diane's right hand.

"Diane and I are getting married." he said

"Congratulations!" Mr. Smith was the first to react. He got up and hugged Timothy, then Diane. Mrs. Smith did the same so also Betty, Mariah and Ashley. It was such a pleasant news. The wedding date had been fixed for December 12th and they had three months to prepare.

The day finally came. It was a proud moment for Mr. Smith. That special moment in a man's life where he walks his daughter down the aisle. His Diane, his pretty shy Diane with dove's eyes was getting married. How wonderful, how marvelous she was also getting married to a young man who he had loved as a son, Timothy his son in the ministry.

As the choir ushered them in with the processional hymn Immortal invincible, the only wise God, Mr. Smith looked at his daughter, a tear fell from his eyes. " you look beautiful my girl."

she smiled " Thank you Father." she replied as they walked in. Diane was dressed in an off shoulder beige white wedding dress. After much debate and tussle, Mariah was chosen as the maid of honour. She also wore a floral embroidered A line dress. She was absolutely stunning. Her sisters also wore the same dress and they all looked beautiful.

Timothy eyes welled up with tears. This was a very special moment for him. Finally he would be comforted. He had found a friend, a confidant, a prayer partner and true love in Diane. He was happy to begin the next phase of his life with her. His mother Lois and grandmother were also here to celebrate with him.The pastor began the ceremony, they took turns to exchange their vows and the groom kissed his wife. It was a done deal,Mr. and Mrs. Timothy Thompson. The whole congratulations cheered. The signing of marriage certificate and recessional hymn soon followed. They went to reception at the Smiths' house. There was lots of dancing, eating and drinking with pictures taken. It was a happy day for everyone and the celebration lasted into the evening.

Timothy and his bride drove off to a resort where they would have their honeymoon.

Chapter Twenty One

Death and resurrection

Mariah prepared Ashley's bed. Lately she had fallen ill again and they had just returned from the hospital. She prepared warm water for Ashley to take her bath. Ashley went into the bathroom but she lingered too long there. Mariah felt uneasy, she got up from the bed and walked to the bathroom. Alas! there was Ashley, she had slumped in the bathtub and laid unconscious.

"Daddy!" Mariah screamed. She dashed out of the room and ran straight to her father's room

Mr. and Mrs. Smith rose up from the bed, terrified by Mariah's scream.

"Ashley! It's Ashley, she is unconscious."

There was no way God was going to fail him a third time. First with the death of his mother and then his wife and now his daughter. The doctors tried to calm him down but he refused to be comforted. As the nurses tried to wheel her body to the morgue, Mr. Smith stopped them.

“No, I'm taking her home.” He insisted

“But she's dead!” the matron said

“No! She's not dead. She will not die but live and declare the works of the Lord.”

“This man is delusional.” Said the Doctor

“I'm fine. I'm fine but I'm not going to bury any piece of me anymore. Timothy let's go.” Mr. Smith said in a Stern voice.

He carried her into his car while Timothy drove home. The news of Ashley's demise had filtered across the neighborhood. Neighbors and church members already lined up in his home but Mr. Smith put them all out.

“I'm not mourning. I'm not mourning.” he said. He carried Ashley to a spare room upstairs and laid her on the bed and cried out to God. He had made up his mind he will neither eat nor drink or sleep until the Lord revived her.

It had been three days but Ashley remained lifeless. Mr. Smith was weary and in great pain. He had laid on her like Elijah, he tried to raise her by the hand like Jairus daughter and Dorcas but after three days, it yielded no result.

Timothy went down to comfort the girls. They had been praying together with Mr. Smith. They had not slept well either. No one went out and no one came in. It was late evening on the third day. Timothy prepared a cup of moringa tea for each of the girls and Mrs. Smith. Soon they all slept. He made a cup of that same moringa tea for himself and Mr. Smith and persuaded him to drink. He drank and soon he was fast asleep. Timothy was about to sip his own tea when a scripture dropped in his heart. Dry bones, Ezekiel 37. Prophecy! prophecy!! The voice echoed continually in his spirit.

Timothy got down on his knees. Mr. Smith had always told him that miracle requires a little effort on their part. Moses had to stretch his rod at the red Sea and lift up his hands for victory. The stone had to be rolled away for Lazarus to come forth. Yes, just a little effort, he has to prophesy, prophesy to Ashley's dry bones. Prophesy to the wilting plant, to the stump that was left. He had to be bold in his God, he began to pray.

"Heavenly father, I thank you for you are committed to touching us and doing wonders. Jesus I thank you because your resurrection power is in us. Holy Spirit I thank you because you are committed to filling us. I commit Sister Ashley into your hands, Let her dry bones come alive! Alive! Awake, oh glory of Ashley. Awake. Awake for your light has come. Rise and live, live and declare the glory of God, live and fulfil the number of your days, live and proclaim the things written about you. For his thoughts for you are good and not evil to give you a future and hope. In Jesus name, Amen. Timothy sat on his chair and sipped his cup of his moringa tea. In no time, he was fast asleep.

It was a warm gentle hand that woke Timothy up. The little hand has been tapping him for a while. Finally the voice spoke.

"Timothy, I'm starving." the voice was weak and frail.

He opened his eyes quickly for he recognized the voice. He was startled to see Ashley standing in front of him.

"Ashley! Ashley...oh my God? Ashley.... Mr. Smith, Mr. Smith. Wake up! Wake up sir!" He shrugged his father violently.Mr. Smith rubbed his sleepy eyes, they were red.

Mr. Smith couldn't believe that he was fast asleep! And even now before his eyes, was Ashley sitting on the bed. He thought he was dreaming. "Timothy!" he called

"Timothy!!" his voice was shaking this time around. "Tell me it's not a dream, speak to me Timothy!" Tears welled up in his eyes. He stood up slowly from the chair and walked closer to Ashley's bed

"Father, she's alive! she's alive!" “See! see!! Look! behold she is alive!” Timothy said.

He rushed and embraced his daughter and he cried aloud. It was so loud that his wife and daughters came to the room

“look! she's alive! she's alive!!” Their father laughed and cried at the same time.

“The girls ran towards their sister and hugged her.”

“I'm hungry Ashley insisted. I want to eat.” she said.

Chapter Twenty Two

Transfer of mantle

Mr. Smith was very old. He no longer travelled for crusades but only preached on Sundays. Timothy took over the weekly services and God added to the church daily. But Timothy had a dream he saw a chariot separating two men as they journeyed. He woke up, having understood the meaning he kept the matter in his heart.

There was a communion service that evening and Timothy's heart was greatly troubled. would it be today? Would the chariot come for him today? Though he was old and stricken, the Evangelist never showed any sign of weakness or feebleness. His eyes were not dim nor his natural vigor diminished. As always, the church was filled and Mr. Smith gave a brief sermon titled "Do this in remembrance of me." The cup of wine was passed round the congregation and unleavened bread shared amongst everyone. Timothy's heart was still heavy, he couldn't share it with anyone not even his wife Diane. He went home to see his wife who had been ill for the past one week. Julian had followed him to check and examine her. After a series of test, she broke the news to the couple. Diane was pregnant. Timothy was so excited that for a moment he forgot the burden of his heart. This is great news! I can't wait to share it with my father, Timothy exclaimed. He thanked Julian very much and offered to drive her home. Diane also accompanied him. Mrs. Smith told them he was resting but Timothy insisted he wanted to see him and she obliged. Timothy knelt by his bedside, He was fast asleep, as he turned to leave, Mr. Smith called on him.

"Timothy my son."

"Yes father." he said turning back and kneeling beside his bed.

"You know the Lord is taking me home today, don't you?"

Timothy wept

"Yes, it's time for me to go. The Lord has done great things for me. He washed me and saved me and gave me a new beginning." He cleared his throat. "He brought my daughters back together and gave them a new start. He delivered Ashley from the bounds of Satan. The Lord has been good to me."

"Yes father, he has been good."

"How I wish he would bless you with the fruit of the womb before I depart." he cried

"Father! don't cry. The Lord your God is ever faithful and he has visited us."

"Really? tell me." he prompted.

"Diane is pregnant. she's six weeks pregnant already!"

"Oh! praise God! praise God! I'm glad. My soul rejoice. Now I can go. He has perfected all things." Mr. Smith struggled to sit up

"What do you want Timothy? ask now before he comes to take me home."

"I want a double of your anointing father." Timothy pleaded.

He laid his right hand on Timothy's head and cried out. "Receive it." there was a small shaking in the room and Timothy landed on the floor. The girls rushed in and their mother too.

"Dear are you alright?" Mrs. Smith asked.

Timothy stood up from the floor.Mr. Smith beckoned on them all to come around.

He held Timothy by his right hand and said to him, Timothy behold your mother, woman behold your son. He placed his wife's hand in Timothy's. He then called on Diane and blessed her saying' may you be fruitful and be fully comforted. Julian came next and he blessed her. May the Lord give you hands that heal, that makes whole and makes the impossible possible. Betty came next and he said, a woman of valor, a woman of steel and a woman of wealth, go and prosper. Mariah came next and for a moment, there was silence, then he spoke. After your heart has wandered away may you find joy in the lord and may He be your strength and everlasting song and to Ashley he said go in the power of his might." A breath heavily and reclined to his bed. He began to sing

I'm pressing on, the upward way,

new heights I gaining everyday..

The others joined him and his voice gradually faded away. Finally, he slept. He slept in the bosom of the Lord. His wife and children weeping and rejoicing.

Chapter Twenty Three

The tributes

The best piece of them was laid in the wooden casket.Diane led the tributes that was made to Mr. Smith.

"My Father was in shambles until he met the Lord. At that time, I had strayed away in my errors, in sin. When I realized it was time to go home, I wasn't sure the kind of reception my Dad would give me.On that fateful night I met my father again, he was waiting for me with open arms and with tears of passion. I could see love in his eyes and I felt comfort in his touch. He carried me like a baby and I knew that I was welcomed home. My father gave me a new start and it was the best moment when he walked me down the aisle. He was a man that loved his family. His wife, his daughters and everyone around him. He preached about heaven, he sang about heaven and now I know he is in heaven. We will miss you father but we know you are in a better city whose builder and maker is God.

A loud applause greeted her tributes and many more people paid tributes to the Evangelist and his remains were committed to mother Earth.

Betty finally had her dream come true, she graduated from the prestigious business school in Victoria city. And as if that wasn't enough, she was now engaged to Brian Dakolo, son of the elegant entrepreneur, Mrs. Dakolo. Mariah also graduated from her school of photography and was employed to be the official photographer of a state governor. Julian worked at the teaching hospital at Yorkville and stayed close to her family. Ashely was freshly admitted into the college of medicine

Timothy and Diane welcomed twin boys whom they named James and John. They were inducted as the head pastor of the church and together they continued the Evangelistic ministry which Mr. Smith had begun. Mrs. Smith lived with the couple and her grandchildren happily and fulfilled.

The End.

About the Author

Olasumbo Ololade Alabi holds a graduate degree in Biochemistry. She is a young dynamic teacher with a unique call to the marriage ministry.

Together with her husband, they are devoted to a ministry of deliverance, Holy spirit baptism and preaching the gospel of Jesus Christ. They are blessed with four children

www.ingramcontent.com/pod-product-compliance
Lightning Source LLC
LaVergne TN
LVHW080040170826
845677LV00025B/1863

* 9 7 9 8 8 4 1 4 0 3 2 4 1 *